WARNING

This book contains sexually explicit scenes and adult language. It may be considered offensive to some readers. This book is for sale to adults ONLY.

* * * * * * * * * * * * * * * *

Please store your files wisely where they cannot be accessed by underage readers.

ISBN-13: 978-1987863482
ISBN-10: 1987863488

Other books by Shyla Starr:

<u>Persuasive Billionaire BWWM Romance Series</u>

Stacey is trying to keep a handle on her life the best that she can. She is on the verge of losing her job and her apartment, while taking care of her sick grandmother. Her life takes an unexpected turn when she meets Charlie, who works for the construction company that is attempting to persuade her to move out of her home.

<u>Tenacious Billionaire BWWM Romance Series</u>

Adalia is too proud to accept help from the billionaire playboy, Trent Dawson. How long can she maintain her resolve? The bank is at her heels to repossess her business. To make matters worse, Adalia finds suspicious evidence of Trent's philandering ways. She must determine whether to trust Trent with the fate of her business and her heart.

<u>Elusive Billionaire Romance Series</u>

Billionaire Hendrick is trying to repair his company's image by putting in some volunteer work, building a school and hospital for the impoverished children in Africa. There, he meets a beautiful African American volunteer, Jocelyn. They hit it off right away but does she belong in his world?

<u>Ardent Billionaire Romance Series</u>

Deirdre doesn't know what to make of the gorgeous man that seems to be interested in her. His name is Parker Walters and he seems friendly enough. There is just something off about him. Why is he trying the hide the fact that he is the heir to his father's billion dollar software empire?

<u>Fervent Billionaire BWWM Romance Series</u>

Alexandra had never been with a white man before. She had seen William at the café before but she always kept her distance. It was unfortunate that their first chance meeting happened when she dropped her breakfast and spilled coffee all over his expensive business suit.

<u>Audacious Billionaire BWWM Romance Series</u>

Chante is torn between staying close to a man beyond her league, and fleeing from him to spare herself from a hopeless position. But she finds she is propelled into a place where she needs to confront her doubts and cast her fate aside to follow the dictates of her heart. Damned if she does and miserable is she doesn't, how will Chante face the events that will lead her to a place of pure happiness or to the pits of a broken heart?

Get the latest update on new releases from the author at:

https://shylastarr.com/newsletter/

This book is Part Two of the "Lonely Billionaire Romance Series"

1 - Love Anew

Tricia was hired to care for billionaire John's wife, who is dying. An unlikely romance emerges after his wife, Rebecca, gives John permission to pursue his happiness after she is gone.

2 - Love Bound

Tricia found herself in another caretaking role. This time, the patient would be her own mother. Her relationship with John was getting complicated. She didn't know whether their feelings for each other were genuine or part of the grieving process from the death of John's wife after a long period of illness. By immersing herself with the task of taking care of her mother, her hope was to forget about John and move on with her life. It didn't hurt that Tricia's best friend's brother, Rod, was a successful and attractive distraction.

3 - Love Decided

John shows up at Tricia's doorstep to finish what they had started. Unsure of what to do but still having real feelings for him, she accepts his invitation for dinner. While at the rodeo with John, Tricia bumps into Rod, the man that she has started to develop feelings for. With two men vying for her affection, Tricia is left with a difficult decision.

Lonely Billionaire Romance Series

Love Bound

Book Two

By Shyla Starr

Copyright Revelry Publishing 2015

Table of Contents

Chapter One

TRICIA SAT in her childhood home and gazed at the wall; today had been particularly trying. In addition to flying from Seattle to Dallas, she had immediately started to take care of her mother. Diagnosed with Alzheimer's, her mother also had a heart condition, and like always, had refused to take any medicine. Before she had moved to Texas, her mother had lived in Alabama where she saw the effects of the Tuskegee Experiment that lasted long after the experiment had officially ended. African-American men who were diagnosed with syphilis in the 1930s were tracked for forty years to see the long-term effects of the disease. Even when a cure came out in the 1950s, the doctors had not cured the men. Instead, they told patients who wanted to be treated that they had already been given medicine. Hundreds and thousands of people from the families were infected and affected by the trial.

Due to this, Tricia's mother refused to listen to white doctors. The crotchety old woman refused to believe that medicine would help or that anything was wrong with her. After an hour of trying and failing to convince her mother to take the medicine, Tricia had finally given up. She had made some bread pudding with dinner and sprinkled crumbled tablets into her mother's portions. It may not have been the most honest solution, but it worked. Now, Tricia was just exhausted.

Moving back to the kitchen, she started to make herself a cup of chamomile tea. With her mother in bed, it was time to drink some tea and unwind. Thankfully, she only had another two days until the weekend. Her brother Tyrone had promised to take care of her mother over the weekend so that Tricia could take a break and catch up with some old friends.

Sipping her cup of tea, she went to the bathroom and turned on the bathwater. As bubbles and warm water filled the tub, she slowly began to remove her clothes. Only a few days ago, she had left John. After telling him of her decision to return home to her mother, she had not talked to him or seen him again. Their brief fling had been as passionate as it was short-lived. She had taken care of his wife during the final stages of ALS. Although they had tried to stop their sexual desires from taking over, John and Tricia had made love more than a couple of times. It was wrong and she still felt guilty. Despite her ethical concerns, she found herself wishing that she was still with him. His confident nature and unwavering conscience had attracted her to him from the moment they met.

Easing herself into the water, Tricia laughed to herself. If only her mother knew that she had slept with a rich, white man. She would never forgive her. Tricia picked up Jane Eyre and tried to read, but even her favorite novel could not distract her mind. She wanted John more than anything. It was impossible for her to go without sex anymore. After realizing how fulfilling and satisfying sex could be with him, she was not willing to go back to her normal celibate lifestyle. She glanced at the bathroom door and saw that it was locked. Moving her hand down her body, she closed her eyes and pretended that her hand was John's. Tricia ran her fingertips around the dark cocoa-colored skin around her nipples and then drew it down further. Initially, she started playing with the soft lips around her clit. This was not enough to satisfy her for long. She moved her clit in slow circles as she imagined John entering her for the first time in the office. The sex had been so magnetic, so electrically charged. She imagined his hard muscles moving against her and moaned.

The moan startled her. She looked at the door to see if her mother had heard anything. There were no sounds from the rest of the house. Moving her hand down along her body again, she moved her fingers faster and faster. Tricia could feel herself approaching orgasm when a sudden sound surprised her. The shrill ringing of the phone pierced the air. For a moment, Tricia thought about ignoring it and finishing herself off. With a belabored sigh, she stood up and grabbed a towel. It could be someone important for her mother.

Exiting the bathroom, she rushed to reach the phone before it stopped ringing. "Hello?" she said with a breathy voice. Holding the phone away from her mouth, she took a deep breath to slow her heart rate down.

The voice on the other end was high-pitched and ecstatic. "Tricia! I can't believe that you are finally home!"

"Oh," Tricia cursed herself. It was just her best friend, Tenaya. They had grown up and gone to school together. Although she was glad to hear from her, she also wished that she had just ignored the phone and called back later. She tried to make her voice sound happier than she was. "Hey, Tenaya. How is everything?"

"Everything is just great. I started working for a new school and really love the other teachers. Your brother told me that you were back, but I just could not believe it. How could you not call me the moment that you returned home?" Tenaya's voice had a teasing quality to it that made Tricia smile.

"I am so sorry. I was going to call immediately, but spent the first few hours trying to convince my mom that she should take her medication."

"She still thinks that the white doctor is lying to her?" Tenaya laughed. Some things never changed.

Tricia rolled her eyes. "You know how she is," she paused. "So what's new with you?"

For the next 20 minutes, Tricia caught up with Tenaya on the phone. Finally it was decided that she would come over on Saturday night for dinner and a romantic comedy marathon. Hanging up the phone, Tricia heaved a sigh of relief. At least one part of her life was going well.

Chapter Two

Tricia tossed the bottle of pills to Tyrone. "Remember," she said. "You need to crumble this up in her food. She will not touch it otherwise. Oh, and make sure she actually eats all of her food. She has developed a bad habit of feeding some of her food to the dog. And..." she looked around as if trying to think of the last thing to tell him.

Tyrone held up his hand to stop her from continuing. "Look, I got it. I can handle this. Just go enjoy yourself. You work hard enough. I don't want to see you back until the wee hours of the morning." He hugged her. "Be safe, little sister."

Smiling, Tricia picked up her purse and left the house. She was finally getting to have some fun. When she was working for John and Rebecca, she had spent most of her evenings sitting at home. With her busy work schedule, she had never really had time to make friends. Maybe returning home was a good thing after all.

Knocking on the door, Tricia nearly fell over as Tenaya tackled her with a bear hug. "I can't believe that you are finally here!" she exclaimed. "Tell me everything, girl!"

Walking inside the house, Tricia started to speak and stopped mid-sentence. Standing before her was the towering figure of Rod. As Tenaya's older brother, Rod had grudgingly let them tag along to the movies and shopping mall. Tricia had had a crush on him as a girl, but was never more to him than his little sister's friend. When she left to go to nursing school, Rod was already studying in college. Apparently, he had grown up well. His buttoned up shirt fit tightly across his bulging chest muscles and he was at least six inches taller than in high school.

Tenaya glanced over at Tricia. "Oh, I forgot to ask. Is it all right if Rod has dinner with us? I figured you may want to spend some time catching up with him as well."

Tricia nodded, unable to speak. Rod smiled. "How are you doing, Tricia? You aren't a little girl in pigtails anymore, I see."

Regaining her ability to speak, Tricia laughed. "And you have grown up a bit, too. How are you doing?"

Rod shrugged. "Fairly good. After college, I decided to get my real estate license. I've been working on some projects to help gentrify the neighborhood."

Her eyes brightened. "I was wondering what was going on. A lot of the stores seem to be coming back."

He nodded. "It takes time, but slowly things will change. Just gotta keep hoping and working toward the goal."

Smiling, Tenaya put her arm around Tricia and brought her toward the kitchen. Calling over the shoulder for Rod to check the mail, she whispered in Tricia's ear. "What was that with you guys? Do you like him?"

Tricia blushed. Had she been that obvious in checking him out? She shook her head.

Giggling, Tenaya wagged her finger at Tricia. "I know when you are crushing on someone. Here, I'll talk to him after you leave and see about getting you a date."

"No, you do not need to do that. He probably doesn't even notice me." Tricia tried to convince Tenaya that she did not need her help in getting a date, but nothing she said changed her mind. Sitting down at the table, Tenaya spooned out some collard greens, baked beans, corn bread and ham.

"Did you miss eating southern food up in Seattle? What do they eat there anyway? Tree bark and granola?" Tenaya laughed good-naturedly.

Rolling her eyes, Tricia took some more corn bread. "No, they do not eat tree bark, although there was a lot of granola in the stores. I don't know. I guess I just ate whatever the chef made."

Rod's eyebrows shot up as he walked into the kitchen and sat down at the table. "A chef? How did you get your own chef?"

Tricia had both siblings looking at her now. "Well, it was not my chef. John and Rebecca had a chef and servants to run the house."

"Huh," Tenaya said. "So you lived pretty well. What made you leave? With the money you made, you could have just hired a nurse."

Tricia shook her head. "No, I needed to be here for my mom."

"But Tyrone is here. Did you just hate the boss? Was he mean?"

Blushing slightly, Tricia focused on eating a bite of baked beans. She did not want to talk about John. Tenaya knew her well enough to figure out what had gone on between them. "No, it was fine," she said. Glancing up, she motioned over to Tenaya. "How's teaching going?"

Tenaya rolled her eyes. She knew that Tricia was changing the subject, but did not want to press the matter with Rod here. "It is going pretty well. Since it is the start of the school year, I have been just trying to put the fear of God into my students. So far, it seems to be working. They have not been acting up too much and seem to actually be doing pretty well with the latest book report."

Before long, dinner was over. Rod stood up to clear the table. "As soon as I wash these dishes for you, I will head out. I got a meeting with a client and I suspect that you ladies need some girl time." Turning to the sink, he began to wash the dishes. After thanking him, Tricia and Tenaya went to the living room.

Plopping down on the couch, Tenaya looked over at Tricia. "So tell me."

Tricia was taken back. She had hoped Tenaya did not notice her blushing earlier. "Tell you what?"

"You know," Tenaya needled her in the ribs. "What was with your bosses? Did they beat you? Forget to pay? Harass you? You were avoiding the subject during dinner."

Shrugging her shoulders, Tricia tried not to say anything. Another sharp look from Tenaya told her that it would not be that easy to change the subject this time. "Fine, Fine. You win. I slept with him."

Tenaya squealed. "Oh my god! You did what? With the billionaire? The guy with his own chef?" Her grip on one of the couch's pillows tightened with excitement. "Oh! Tell me! How was it?"

Tricia smiled. If she was going to share her secret with anyone, it might as well be Tenaya. "It was... amazing. But more than just the sex, there was this feeling that it could have become something more."

Frowning, Tenaya thought for a moment. "But why would you ever leave then? If you thought it could be love someday, why didn't you try to make it work?"

Tricia shook her head. "I can't. What would everyone think? What would I think? The poor black girl from the 'hood dating the billionaire? At best, they would think that he was taking advantage of me. At worst, everyone would say that I am a gold digger. Not to mention, could you imagine the reaction? He may be just a businessman, but John's money has attracted the tabloid more than once in the past. If he was with a black girl, every newspaper in the country would pick up that story. The country is getting more liberal, but there are still people who are against an interracial couple."

Tenaya laughed. "Like your mother, for one. But really, what if he was the one? Couldn't you have at least tried staying with him just to see? You could have just let your true love go."

Shaking her head, Tricia patted Tenaya on the hand. "You are a hopeless romantic. This is not one of your romantic comedies; it is my life. If I screw up, I cannot just push rewind. Do you really think that there is just one true love for each person?"

Tenaya nodded her head with conviction. "Yes, I do."

"Well, when you find your true love, I will try dating John. Until then, let me live my own private life. Besides, you were trying to hook me up with your brother just twenty minutes ago." Tricia laughed. "You are truly incorrigible. Here, pick out a movie and I will make us some popcorn." Realizing that the topic was over, Tenaya settled in for a long night of romantic movies.

Arriving home around midnight, Tricia slid her key in the lock. As she walked into the entryway, she caught sight of some flowers on the table with a card. Confused, she opened the envelope. Inside was a note from Rod with his number. Along with his number, the message read, "Call me tomorrow if you are interested in going on a date tomorrow night. Dress up and we will take the town by storm." Smiling, she put the card back in the envelope. She would call him in the morning. It would be good for her to see someone other than John.

Chapter Three

Stepping out of the shower, Tricia slipped into a black thong and garters. Fastening a matching bra, she stepped into a bright red dress. The vivid red color contrasted perfectly with her dark skin. As she applied makeup, she realized that she was actually getting nervous. Initially, she had not worried too much about the date. Still wrapped up in John, she had figured that this date would just serve as a welcome distraction. But as the date approached, she found herself becoming increasingly nervous.

The sound of the doorbell disrupted her musings. He was early. Thankfully, she had started getting ready far sooner than she needed to. Spraying on some perfume, she slipped into red heels and went to answer the door. In front of her, Rod was dressed in a black suit and tie. She raised an eyebrow. "Exactly how dressed up should I be?" she asked.

Rod smiled and she felt herself grow weak in her knees. He was so terribly attractive. He shook his head. "What you are wearing is perfect. You look unbelievably stunning."

Walking her to the car, he opened her door. Unable to think of anything to say, she just thanked him and he started the car. "So... where are we going?" she asked.

"I have a reservation at the Five Sixty restaurant in Reunion Tower," he said. She raised her eyebrows. Reunion Tower was an iconic part of the Dallas skyline. It was essentially a giant ball that rotated at the top of a building. From the restaurant, people could see the whole city while they ate. Getting a reservation would have been difficult and exceptionally expensive.

"I am guessing that the real estate business is going well," she said.

In response, Rod laughed. "I suppose it is. Honestly, I just figured you deserved a treat after the last few weeks. Tenaya told me that the patient you were taking care of ended up dying recently. I can't imagine that this past month has been easy for you at all."

Tricia shook her head. If only he knew. "No, it really has not been a good month." She paused. If Tenaya told him about Rebecca's death, what else could she have said? "So, what else did Tenaya tell you?" she asked Rod.

Shrugging, Rod patted her hand reassuringly. "Not too much. I tried pumping her for information, but she said I should get to know you on my own instead of cheating."

"Sounds like her," Tricia laughingly responded in relief. She was not ready to talk about John with Rod. Honestly, she may never tell him about John. There was no reason for him to become jealous or worry about another guy, especially at this point in the relationship.

After finally locating a parking spot and getting into the building, Tricia and Rod waited to be shown to their table. As they walked across the restaurant, Tricia gasped in surprise. "It is so beautiful!"

Rod glanced over at her. "Wait, have you never been here?"

"Never. I always wanted to go, but it seemed like such a waste of money when I was a student. After I graduated, there was just never time on my visits to Mom."

Smiling, Rod slid his arm around her waist and pulled her close. "Well, I am glad that I get to be your first then. The food is actually as good as the view, so I think you are going to have an excellent time."

Sitting at the table, Tricia let Rod order for her. Half the menu items were written in completely unintelligible French. While he ordered, Tricia relaxed and let the French phrases roll over her. After the waiter left, she looked over at Rod. "So tell me, how do you know how to order here? It isn't really a talent that you would learn in the old neighborhood."

Lifting his glass to her, Rod took a sip of wine. "True, but there are always other ways. I studied in France during college. My time there was fortunate because I often take out-of-town investors here to go over bids and potential projects."

Tricia smiled. "You are a truly interesting person. If I get to know you better, will I continue to uncover new layers to your personality?"

Rod shrugged. "I suppose so, but I really think that is true for everyone." He started to say more, but the first course had arrived. Falling silent for a moment, the pair waited for the waiter to leave before resuming their conversation. Tricia was surprised. Unlike most first dates, spending time with Rod felt so natural. She felt completely comfortable around him and the conversation flowed through dinner. By the time the check came, she found herself unusually sad. This wonderful evening was about to come to an end.

Standing up from the table, Tricia let Rod hold her around the waist again as they left. It felt so different being with him. Unlike John, she did not have to hide their blossoming relationship or worry about the reaction of other people. Anyone in the restaurant would just see an attractive black couple if they looked over.

Arriving at the car, Tricia hesitated for a moment. "What is it?" Rod asked.

She shook her head. "I am not sure. I just realized that I really do not want this evening to be over." Beyond enjoying the evening, she found herself wanting to bring him home with her. She had never managed to reach orgasm the other day and really needed to have sex.

Rod smiled widely. "Well, we can always go somewhere else. Where do you want to go?"

Perhaps it was the wine or perhaps she was far more confident than she thought. No matter what the reason was, she was as surprised as Rod by the next sentence that came out of her mouth. "What if we check into a hotel?"

Stunned, Rod did not say anything for a moment. Tricia blushed deeply and shook her head. "Sorry, forget I said that."

Shaking his head, Rod slammed the door of the car and pushed her against it. Pressing his body against hers, he tilted her head up to his and kissed her. The kiss was long and passionate. Pulling away, he kept his eyes locked on hers. She could feel his pulse beating fast against hers. Rod kissed her again. "Yes, we can do that. I was just surprised. I would love to find a hotel."

Getting in the car, he held her hand in his. Now that she had asked him to go to a hotel, he did not know what to say. Throughout the evening, Rod had fantasized about sleeping with her. He had imagined how her breasts would look and what her legs would feel like wrapped around his. Now that this was actually happening, he was dumbfounded. In the seat next to him, Tricia was silent as well. She could not believe that she had been so forward, but she also did not regret it. She wanted this to happen.

Checking into the hotel, Tricia and Rod walked hand in hand up the stairs. Between them was an unspoken agreement not to talk about what was about to happen. It seemed as even a word that suggested the coming pleasure would break the spell. Self-conscious and restrained, Rod unlocked the door and stepped back to let Tricia through.

The door shut and Tricia was left staring at Rod. Neither of them was able to make a move. Before Rod, was a vision in red that could be all his in an instant. The thrill of the coming sexual encounter overwhelmed him. He pulled out a pocket knife. Tricia raised an eyebrow. "What is that for?"

He looked down at the knife and seemed almost surprised to see it. "I want... I want to cut your dress off of you and see your breasts pop out and expose the entirety of your body." Rod fell silent as he finished talking. Some type of strange desire was taking control of him and he had no clue what he was doing. It was like an entirely different person existed within him who had taken control.

Tricia nodded. Demurely, she lay back on the bed. Her long chocolate legs stretched endlessly toward Rod. Groaning with pent-up desire, he stepped toward her. Grasping the top of her dress in his hand, he ripped straight down the middle with his pocket knife. As the sides of the dress fell, her breasts bounced pleasingly out. Perfectly round and well-shaped, her nipples were hard enough to see through her bra. Rod lifted her legs and pushed her back farther on the bed. Reaching between her legs, he felt her cunt and realized how wet she was. At the moment he touched her, Tricia moaned. She had been waiting for this for days. Tricia no longer cared about her reputation or about what Rod may think of her. If he was not inside of her soon, she would explode.

Rocking her hips upward, she felt his fingers go in her. Swirling around inside of her body, she immediately realized that this was not enough. All it did was tease her and make her want him more. Tricia sat up and wrapped her legs around his lower body. Reaching her hands up, she clasped his neck and pulled him down. "I need you," she whispered. The sound of her sultry, soft voice drove him to madness. Pulling off his pants in a clean motion, he entered her immediately. There was no time to get a condom, ask about birth control or see if she wanted sex. He had to have her now. Pressing her wrists into the bed, he thrust as hard as he could into her. The pain brought tears to her eyes, but she enjoyed it. She wanted it rough and wanted to feel the full force of him inside her. Arching her back, she brought her hips up against his. This sexualized motion brought him close to orgasm instantly. Gasping, he grabbed her hips with his hands.

"Not yet," he said. "You do not get to have your way yet." Leaning back on his heels, he brought her onto his lap without pulling out of her. With her weight above him, gravity caused him to enter even deeper inside her. The supreme pleasure caused her to cry out.

"Don't," she cried, "Don't stop." Tricia tried to move her hips against his, but he held her body tightly. Like a wild animal, she worked on moving against his body. Again and again, he rebutted her advances. Tricia's rising sexual frustration turned him on and he wanted to make her wait. Finally, he released her. Shoving him back down onto the bed, she put her hands behind her on his knees. Arching backwards, she managed to get the entire length of his cock into her body. Gasping in pleasure, she moved her hips hard against his. All of her inhibitions had left her entirely and she cried out in pleasure as she felt her orgasm approaching. As the bright ecstasy of orgasm passed through her body, a brief glimpse of Rod's face told her that he was orgasming as well. Sweaty and flushed, the pair fell back on the bed.

She rolled over to look at him. "That was amazing. Do you want...?"

Rod smiled. "Again? Of course." He grabbed his tie from the ground. "Tie me to the chair first. I like it when you take control." He kissed the inside of her wrist gently. "It is unbelievably sexy." Moving to the chair, he waited patiently for her to come to him. This was going to be a long, but pleasurable, night.

Moving over to the chair, Tricia smiled wickedly. Her eyes gleamed brightly in the dim light. Kneeling behind the chair, she tied his body tightly. His hands were unable to move at all.

Returning to the bed, she searched the covers for Rod's pocket knife. Finding it, she went back to Rod. She flicked out the blade and ran it against his skin. Tracing his nipple with the tip of the blade, she cut a hair off by accident.

Leaning close to him, she whispered in his ear. "Too close?" she asked.

He shook his head. "Use me as you wish."

Tricia ran the knife down his body and allowed it to gently press against his cock. The sudden attention caused him to harden. As he became hard, his cock came closer to the motionless knife. Groaning in agony, he tried to think of anything that would make him less turned on. Smiling, Tricia pulled the knife away. The instant it was gone, his cock jerked back to attention. Trembling with anticipation, Rod moaned. "Please, please, don't keep teasing me like this."

Tricia smiled. "If you think you want me now, just wait." Sitting down on the bed, she spread her legs and started to touch herself. From across the room, Rod struggled to get a clear view. Each time he tried to look, the soft pink folds of her lips were out of sight. Minutes passed in agonizing succession as he waited for her to stop teasing him so badly. Finally, she came over to him on the chair. Straddling her body across his, she sank down without warning on his cock. The slick wetness welcomed him deep inside her and the sudden pleasure brought him close to orgasm. Gasping, he tried to move away. "I can't. You have teased me for too long. I won't be able to hold back."

Grinning, Tricia leaned down to bite his nipple. Straightening her body again, she moved her hips violently against his. The motion set his entire body trembling as he struggled to control himself. "You better hold back or I will whip you later."

The thought of her running a whip along his body was too much. Precum seeped from him as he used every mental technique possible to hold back. Tricia did not help it. Seduced by the power, she wanted to watch his agony as he tried not to orgasm. Moving her hips rhythmically, she lifted them with each repetition so his cock was fully removed before it entered her again. As she sought to tease him further, a surprise feeling started to blossom within her. She was close to orgasm as well. Unable to tease any longer, her control completely weakened. She found herself thrusting her body against his in wanton abandon. As he slid into her, each nerve ending in her body was set on fire with a passion so intense it clouded her entire mind. Conscious thoughts left her and she threw herself into him. Harder and harder she forced her cunt against him until he broke. Throbbing and jerking madly, he came inside of her and filled her completely. The throbbing of his cock struck some deep, evolutionary force within her and she came. Her muscles and tendons convulsed throughout her entire body. The strength of her orgasm caused her leg to cramp, but she could not stop moving against him. The pleasure was too intense and unreal for her to ever want to stop. Finally, the sensation became too overpowering. As her orgasm ended, she pulled her body off of his and reluctantly untied him. Even the simple act of unfastening his bonds reminded her again of what she wanted. Rod was in for an even longer night.

Chapter Four

Several months passed quickly in succession. The romance with Rod was quickly picking up speed. In addition to mind-blowing sex, Tricia was quickly discovering the many facets of his personality. On weekends, Rod coached a basketball team at the youth center and he secretly enjoyed gardening. Every day, it seemed like Tricia was learning new things about him. She could not believe how lucky she was to finally find someone who was just right for her. Her relationship with Rod was not the only good luck she had. Recently, Tyrone had moved back into their mother's house. This meant that Tricia could have more evenings off. At first, she had avoided telling Tyrone about Rod because she did not know where the relationship was going. He figured out on his own a few weeks previously and Tricia found herself not caring. At last, she was in a healthy relationship.

Humming as she went into the bedroom, Tricia set down the breakfast tray. Reaching over, she shook her mother's arm. How strange. Normally, her mother would wake up as soon as the sun was up. Her mother did not respond. Shaking her arm again, Tricia was met with no reaction. Horrified, she took her pulse. She could not feel anything. Reaching for the phone, she dialed 911 with a shaky hand. Telling the operator her address, she told them to come quick. Her mother may be dead.

As she waited for the ambulance, Tricia sank down to the ground. Her mother had been doing better. Her Alzheimer's was not improving, but it also was not getting worse. She had even been taking her heart medication willingly. Unless... Tricia frowned and rushed to look in her mother's dresser drawer. Tossing the clothes out, she finally found what she had been searching for. A small jewelry box in her mother's dresser was full of pills. She had been slipping them out of her mouth when Tricia was not looking.

Stepping back in horror, Tricia fell against the wall again. Sliding down into a squatting position, she hung her head in her hands. Sobs racked her body. She had known that her mother was sick, but death had always seemed like a faraway, unreal outcome.

A knock was heard and Tricia stood up to let the paramedics in. People and a flurry of equipment passed around her. As the paramedics tested her mother's pulse and checked for any signs of breathing, the room became increasingly gloomy. It did not seem like her mother was ever going to come back from this. Finally, the dreaded moment came when one of the paramedics looked up and shook his head. "I'm sorry," was all that he said.

Tricia ran out of the room. She could not be there. The entire world seemed to be closing in around her and suffocating her. She had to go somewhere or do something. If she went to sleep, maybe she would wake up and realize that this was a dream.

Leaving the house, she shuffled along. For once, the fall rain was just a light drizzle instead of a downpour. As she thought disconnectedly about this one bright side, she heard a crash of thunder. Texas's normal torrential rain started up and she was drenched in moments. As normal people sought cover or pulled out umbrellas, Tricia kept walking. The rain matched her mood. In the coldness and the stinging rain, she found the same physical sensations that she was feeling within her. A cold emptiness filled her soul and made it impossible for her to think. This year had been filled with too much stress and too much death. She needed out.

Back at the house, Tyrone had arrived home to discover the paramedics taking his mother to a funeral home. Sinking down into the couch, he waited while they relayed what had happened with his sister. Despite his pain, Tyrone managed to think about his sister. She needed help. Calling up Rod, he explained the situation in as few words as he could. As soon as Rod heard what the problem was, he immediately told Tyrone that he would find her and make everything right again. Hitting the streets in his car, he drove up and down each road in search of her. Some of the low-lying streets had already started to flood, but Rod drove straight through them.

Rounding the corner, Rod caught sight of her shivering under an awning. Pulling up the car, he jumped out and pulled off his jacket. Wrapping it around her, he brought Tricia to the car and sat her down. She was completely senseless. As he started to drive, he kept glancing over at her with worry in his eyes. Tricia was completely falling apart. Rod drove to her house and packed a bag for her as she sat motionless on the couch. Calling the office, he told them that he was going to take a few days off. He needed to take her somewhere away from the grief and let her recover.

Getting back in the car, he drove silently to the town of Muenster. An hour away from Dallas, the German village was a completely different setting and may help her recover from her sudden shock. As soon as he checked into the hotel room, Tricia fell onto the bed and passed out.

For several days, Rod stayed with her in the room. With brief breaks for crying, Tricia spent the entire time sleeping. Finally one morning, she woke up and sat up in the bed. Her eyes seemed clearer than they had been for days.

Looking up from his book, Rod smiled gently. "Are you okay now?" he asked. His voice had a soft note of concern.

Tricia stretched wearily. "How long have I been out?"

Rod stepped over to the bed and sat down next to her. "You have been asleep or catatonic for about two days. I thought a change of pace could help you feel better. Did I do the right thing?"

Tricia stood up and looked out the window. Bewildered, she turned around. "Where in the world did you take me?" The Bavarian-style houses were completely foreign to her.

Laughing, Rod stepped behind her and wrapped his arms around her shoulders. "You're still in Texas, my dear. We're just in Muenster."

Tricia turned. The enormity of what he had done for her came crashing down. "So you waited with me for two days? Why? You did not have to do that. My brother would have taken care of me."

Rod kissed the back of her head. "Your brother could have, but I wanted to. I love you, Tricia."

She turned to look at him and was unable to think of anything to say. He had never told her that he loved her before. "You love me?"

Rod nodded. "I was going to make some grand romantic gesture and then tell you, but now seemed like the right time." He held her closer. Gradually, he realized that she had not said anything in return. "Wait, you never responded. Do you…" he paused and tried again. "Do you love me, too?"

Tricia did not know what to say. She did not know if she loved him. Honestly, she had put off the thought of a future relationship. She had enjoyed living in the present and taking each date as it arrived. Turning to face him, she ran her hand along his face gently. "I don't really know right now. There is far too much for me to take in. I need to deal with the loss of my mother before I can really think about anything else. When I do say that I love you, you will be able to know that I mean it though."

Rod tried to hide his disappointment and turned to start packing. "It's okay, Tricia. You are right. I should not have sprung this on you. Don't worry about it for now. I just want to help you get through this."

Picking up the suitcases, Rod left the hotel room to put them in the car. From the window, Tricia watched him walk across the parking lot. Was she so heartless for not loving him? She really did not know how she felt about anything right now. Sighing, she walked into the bathroom and managed to find a complimentary toothbrush. By the time Rod returned, she had showered and brushed her teeth. She was finally starting to feel a lot more normal.

The ride home was completely silent. Neither partner could think of anything to say that did not involve their relationship or feelings for each other. After a ride that seemed like it stretched on for years, Rod finally pulled in front of Tricia's house. Helping her out of the car, he wheeled her suitcase to the door for her. Kissing her gently on the forehead, he returned to the car and left Tricia to face the house on her own. For several moments, she stood silently in front of the closed door. If she went inside, she would have to face a house that no longer held her mother. She would have to start packing her mother's things and look into preparing for the funeral. Even worse, she would have to face a stream of questions from her brother about how she was doing.

Sighing deeply, she finally pushed the key into the lock. Stepping into the entryway, she fumbled for the light switch in the dark. As the light flipped on, she caught sight of some roses on the entryway table. Frowning slightly, she let out a sigh of exasperation. Rod just could not leave it alone. Adding flowers to his sudden confession of love was too much. The extra attention only served to cause more stress for her.

Reaching for the flowers, she brought them into the kitchen to throw them away. At the last moment, she decided to open the card. He deserved to at least have the card read. Slipping the card out, her jaw dropped. The flowers were not from Rod. They were from John. In his block writing, he had scrawled out a happy birthday note to her. Tricia smiled wanly. She had completely forgotten that her birthday was today. Her brother must have accepted these flowers for her.

Sitting down at the kitchen table, she scrutinized the note. It said that John would be in town next week. He would be dealing with business, but wanted to meet her for business if she was available. On the note, he had left a number for her to call.

Pressing the note to her chest, Tricia shut her eyes. What was she supposed to do? She had not thought about John for weeks. Every time she had sex with Rod, her feelings for John had slowly started to dissipate. Now, he had shoved his way back into her life. She did not know what to do. With Rod, the sex was amazing and the relationship made sense. John would never be an easy person to have a relationship with, but she connected with him on a totally different level.

Leaning back in the chair, Tricia realized she had another problem. Rod was Tenaya's brother. If she hurt Rod, Tenaya would never forgive her. Ironically, seeing John may not even matter. By not loving him fully, she had already hurt him. For several long minutes, she sat indecisively. She wanted to see John so badly, but it went against everything that she felt was right. Impulsively, she reached for the phone and dialed. She did not care what was right. She wanted to see John again.

-To be continued in Book 3-

If you enjoyed this title, I would appreciate your leaving a review of the book. Good reviews encourage an author to write as well as help books to sell. Good reviews can be just a few short sentences describing what you liked about the book without having a spoiler. If you could spend 30 seconds writing a review, I would appreciate it: you can review this title right now at your favorite retailer.

Here is a preview of the **next book** you may also enjoy:

Love Decided - Lonely Billionaire Romance Series, Book 3

TRICIA WAITED impatiently at the door. Her hands were shaking with nervous tension. It had taken an unbelievable amount of time to do her makeup because her hands kept jerking as she tried to apply lipstick and mascara. Finally, it seemed like it was almost time for John to arrive. Trying to calm her nerves, she sat down on the couch.

Although it seemed like forever ago, Tricia had once been in love with John. Despite their better intentions, they had succumbed to an animalistic desire and had sex—more times than she could count. Tricia had been nursing his sick wife, Rebecca, until she died. After Rebecca's death, Tricia had returned home and taken care of her mother. Now, it seemed like anything was possible. After burying her mother, John had sent her a message and flowers for her birthday. She was going to have dinner with him tonight.

Tricia smoothed her dress awkwardly. She had worn this red dress not long before she had finally had sex with John for the first time. Although she had pretended not to notice, she had seen him watching her slim curves move and strain against the fabric. She cursed herself silently. How could she possibly be trying to dress up for him? Since Tricia had returned home, she had dated Rod. Attractive and successful, Rod was a wealthy real estate developer. More importantly, he was kind, funny and actually black. Although times were changing, dating someone of the same race would still make her life easier. Ruining things with Rod would be terrible. He was her best friend, Tenaya's, brother and she would probably lose her friend as well as her boyfriend.

Standing up, Tricia walked over to the phone. She wanted to call John and tell him that she could not make it. Being around John would be an impossible temptation for her. Dialing the phone number, she waited until his voicemail picked it up. Unwilling to cancel a date with a message, she went over to the couch to sit down again. Before she could get comfortable, she heard a knock at the door.

Groaning, she managed to smile before she pulled the door open. In front of her, John stood with a handful of red roses. Smiling widely, he made a move toward her and seemed prepared to sweep her off her feet in an instant. Pushing his hand away, she gave him a hug.

Confused, John hugged her before stepping back. "You look... ravishing, Tricia. How are you?" In his voice, she could hear the unspoken question. He did not know about Rod and could not understand her hesitation.

"I'm good, John. For a while, I was confused and depressed after my mother's death. Fortunately, Rod was there to help me through it." As soon as she said this, she regretted it. Tricia had wanted to slip Rod's name in so that John would know she had a boyfriend. John's crestfallen expression made her instantly reconsider this decision. "Here, come in, come in. I can get you a cup of tea or something before we go. Did you want anything?"

If you enjoyed this sample then look for **Love Decided - Lonely Billionaire Romance Series, Book 3.**

Here is a preview of **another book** you may also enjoy:

ALEXA STARED at the bright white of the computer screen. It seemed to be mocking her with its very emptiness. She sighed. If she did not start on her freelance work soon, she would never get done. With a groan, she stood up and went to the kitchen for a cup of coffee. She decided to take a much-needed break before she started the workday. Alexa glanced at the clock. Already, it was approaching ten in the morning. Today was a waste. All she needed to do was look up the keywords needed for a client's blog. That was it. Leaning back against the counter, she tried to refocus her mind on work. Nothing helped. Since her fling with William a month ago, she had been unable to focus on anything. It was amazing that one little date could change her entire outlook.

The ringing of the phone snapped her back to the present. Crossing the room, she picked it up and answered. The number was not familiar, but many of the clients she used called her on this line. It could be important or it could be a spammer. In her line of work, either option was equally likely.

"Hello?" she asked. "Alexandria Enterprise. How may I direct your call?"

A laugh was heard on the other end of the line and Alexa groaned. It was her mother. "Now don't you Alexandria me, young lady. I gave birth to you and I know as well as anybody that you are no Alexandria."

Alexa rolled her eyes. Vividly alive and slightly domineering, her mother was a veritable force of nature. Alexa had named her company Alexandria as a reference to the old libraries that burned in Alexandria. The metaphor was lost on her mother, however. "Yes, Mama, I know. Ten hours of labor and what did you get?"

"A daughter who puts on airs," her mother finished.

Alexa sighed. "So what is it this time, Mama? You fixing me up with Sammy again? He's gay, you know. Just because you and his mom don't believe it..." she trailed off. It was useless arguing. Her mother had noticed Alexa's lack of a love life and spent the last month trying to fix her up with men from the neighborhood. Alexa groaned inwardly. Men. No, the men of the neighborhood had been snatched up a long time ago. What was left was a mix of boys who could never compete. The only person she would have even considered dating was Sammy, but he had other interests that did not involve slender hips and voluptuous breasts.

"No, no, Alexa. I won't be fixing you up with anyone this time. I just want to see you every once in a while. Dinner with me tonight? I'll cook your favorite... fried chicken."

Sighing, Alexa nodded. She instantly realized that her mother couldn't see her nod, so she replied, "Sure, Mama. That's fine. I'll see you around six."

Hanging up the phone, Alexa went back to her desk. She would have to complete a great deal of work before driving down to Tacoma. Even worse, she was going to be suckered into eating her mother's extremely delicious and exceptionally fattening chicken. So much for giving up fried food.

After she sat down at the desk, the minutes quickly fled by. Alexa became engrossed in the project and barely noticed that the light was starting to dim from the sky. Glancing up, she realized that it was already 4 PM. Thankfully, she was done. Leaning back from the computer, she reached over and picked her phone on the first ring.

"Hello, Alexandria Enterprises."

"Hey... Alexa? This is you, right?" The voice on the phone caused her to sit up straight. She recognized the deep, gravelly voice.

"William? What... what do you want?" She winced. Her attempt at playing it cool already failed.

"Nothing, Alexa, at least not in the way you're thinking." He paused as he tried to figure out how to word his question. "Well, I remember you talking about marketing and the internet at our... dinner." Alexa did not say anything, so William continued. "Anyhow, I think I may want to utilize your services. When would you be available?"

Alexa picked up her schedule. Normally, she would tell him that she did not work with friends, but considering that they had only spent an evening together, she could ignore her normal rule. Not to mention that he would probably end up being one of her major clients. "Yes, yes, I could do that. How about we arrange for a consultation in..." She flipped through her schedule. "Two weeks?"

"Two weeks? Wow, business must be going well. Yes, we could do that. Let me put my secretary on the line and she will handle the scheduling aspect. I'll tell you more about what I want in person."

If you enjoyed this sample then look for **Love Restrained - Fervent Billionaire BWWM Romance Series, Book 2**.

Here is a preview of **another story** you may enjoy:

"**THEY WANT** them Black Forest cheesecakes done in thirty," Melanie said, chewing on a stick of gum.

Adalia sighed and blinked a couple times. "I'm not a miracle worker. Besides, I hardly think anyone in the store is going to riot if I don't get it out on time."

Annie's Market specialized in nothing but providing loads of baked goods to as many customers as possible – in short, the quality was terrible. The recipes in the bakery section were set and Adalia's creativity was stifled, but a job was a job and God knew she needed the money after that debauchery with Trent.

Melanie shuffled out of the kitchen and the doors swung in her wake. The girl had about as much finesse as a bull on steroids. She'd worked there for a week as Adalia's manager, and it was difficult to respect her.

Failure, failure, failure. The word repeated itself in her head.

Measure out the flour, *failure*, weigh the sugar, *failure*, beat the eggs, *failure*. It didn't matter what she did or which way she looked at things. She'd messed up. Big time.

Melanie shoved back into the kitchen. "Store manager says to get 'em done or you're in trouble."

"You went to the store manager?" Adalia stared at her and shook her head.

"Yeah, and there's some guy here to see you."

Adalia's heart leapt into her throat, and she stopped moving completely. Screw the Black Forest cakes, what if Trent had arrived? Mortification paralyzed her; she was glued to the spot.

The last thing she'd want was the billionaire to see her slumming it in a tiny store bakery.

"Who?" Adalia whispered.

Melanie raised an eyebrow. "Derick or something, I didn't hear proper. Get them cakes ready." She turned and charged out again, still chewing gum like it was her air to breathe.

"Derick," Adalia said to herself, shaking her head in confusion. Who the hell was Derick? She dusted off her hands on her grubby apron and strolled out of the kitchen and into the kiosk area.

It wasn't Derick; it was DeShawn.

"Hey baby," he murmured, resting his elbows on top of the glass case, and gazing into her eyes. "I've been thinking about you all day."

"I'm honored," she replied, and the sarcasm was lost on him. She didn't want to see Trent, but she surely didn't want to see her ex-boyfriend either. He'd pretty much messed with her mind for long enough, and she didn't need that added pressure or drama.

"You working here now?"

"No," she grumbled. "I just come here to work out."

"Huh?"

"Nothing," she said with a sweet smile. "What do you want, DeShawn? I've got things to do right now." She glanced out over the empty store and made eye contact with the manager.

He glared at her and tilted his head to the side like the oversized buzzard he was. "Hurry up," he mouthed then tapped his cheap Kmart watch.

She forced herself not to roll her eyes at the authority figure. Once upon a time, she'd loved baking, but that was when she'd been able to create something from fresh, not stick to the plan, no matter how disgusting it was.

"Baby?" DeShawn's voice interrupted her train of thought.

"What is it?" She snapped her focus back to his face. "Like I said, I'm busy."

"And I said I want you back."

Agony erupted in her chest, pushing aside every other emotion. She'd been through so much, tasted a hint of success and then fallen hard. All she wanted was to get back on her feet and move on with her life, but DeShawn was back.

"Why? Give me one good reason why."

"Because I love you, baby," he said, leaning over the case of day-old cakes to grab at her arm. She didn't jerk it away and he managed to bring it up and take hold of her hand instead. He brought the tips of her fingers to his lips and kissed them gently.

There wasn't heat like there was with Trent, but it still brought out something in her. Something good. A long forgotten memory of what it was like to be touched by a person who cared.

Did DeShawn truly care?

"I don't trust you, and I don't need that," she said, pulling her hand from his grasp and wiping the back on her apron with a sour expression.

"You never gave me a chance to prove myself to you. I love you so much, baby, and you ain't never given me the chance to show it."

"What are you talking about?" she spat, trembling from head to toe. "I gave you every chance in the world to show your love for me and you didn't make any effort whatsoever."

"I came to your daddy's place to talk to you."

"What?!" Adalia laughed out loud and the manager shot her a look of pure loathing. "I'm not talking about after I dumped your sorry ass. By then, it was too late. I'm talking about before. Because when it really mattered, you didn't give a crap."

"I was high a lot of the time."

"Precisely." Adalia gripped the low-slung counter with both hands.

Melanie appeared beside her. "You gotta get back to work. The Black Forest cakes aren't gonna bake themselves."

"What the hell does a store need two managers for?" Adalia blurted, then snapped her mouth shut.

Melanie glared at her for a minute then charged off again, muttering to herself.

That meant more trouble for her. The bakery manager chewed and steamed her way over to the store manager and flung her arms around, describing what Adalia had said in minute detail, apparently.

"You realize how busy I am, right?" Adalia breathed slowly, through the anger and disappointment in herself.

"Yeah, true that. Look, girl, I can't live without you. I'm not gonna treat you bad again. Only give you what you deserve. You gotta believe me."

"No, DeShawn, all I 'gotta' do is work and keep this damn job so I can earn enough money to make rent this damn month."

"So, come live wit' me." DeShawn grinned and spread his arms wide, then scratched beneath the line of his do-rag. His muscles rippled beneath his tank top, but she didn't have that spark with him.

Maybe she'd never feel that chemistry again. Hell, she'd probably imagined it in the first place.

"I'm not moving in with you, DeShawn. There's no question about that in my mind."

"Aight," he said, then rapped his knuckles on the glass counter. "So lemme take you on a date."

The store manager held up a hand to Melanie's face, then walked past her and marched in Adalia's direction.

Some of the shelves in the store leaned skew, the cans had a layer of dust which matched the grime on the front windows. Hardly any sunlight made it through to the back, so the fluorescents buzzing and clicking overhead made perfect sense.

"You need to leave now," Adalia murmured, bracing herself for the complaints from the manager. "I ain't leaving," DeShawn said. The manager, Mr. Hubbard, was almost at the kiosk.

"What?"

"I ain't leaving until you say you'll go on a date with me."

"Do you realize I could lose my job over this? Do you even care?"

"I care about you, but I ain't gonna take no for no answer, and you need to see that, girl." DeShawn seemed oblivious to the risk he'd put her under just by showing up. She was at the end of her tether with him and with everything else.

Mr. Hubbard was steps away.

"Fine, I'll go on a date with you. Just get outta here!" She hissed it at him, then plastered up a broad smile.

"Adalia," Hubbard said, stopping beside DeShawn. "I'd like to see you in the kitchen for a moment."

"Yes, sir," she said, still with that sick, fake smile on her lips. It suited how she felt inside: nauseated by the situation and what she had to do each day. She was a sellout.

"On Friday, baby," DeShawn called out after.

The kitchen doors swung shut behind her.

If you enjoyed this sample then look for **Love Forgiven: Tenacious Billionaire BWWM Romance Series, Book 2**.

Other Books by Shyla Starr

- Persuasive Billionaire BWWM Romance Series

- Tenacious Billionaire BWWM Romance Series

- Elusive Billionaire Romance Series

- Ardent Billionaire Romance Series

- Fervent Billionaire BWWM Romance Series

- Audacious Billionaire BWWM Romance Series

Get the latest update on new releases from the author at:

https://shylastarr.com/newsletter/

About the Author - Shyla Starr

Shyla currently specializes in writing interracial romance stories and is a huge fan of the alpha male. Simply put, there just aren't enough stories about mixed couple romances, which is something she is aiming to fix.

Being a bookworm all her life, when Shyla discovered men she also realized how easy it was to fulfill her fantasies through her writing.

When not writing and fantasizing about men, Shyla enjoys dancing, reading and chilling with her friends.

Connect with Shyla Starr

I really appreciate you reading my book! Here are my social media coordinates:

Friend me on Facebook: https://www.facebook.com/shylastarrauthor

Follow me on Twitter: https://twitter.com/shylstarr

Check me out on Goodreads: https://www.goodreads.com/author/show/8436084.Shyla_Starr

Subscribe to my newsletter: https://shylastarr.com/newsletter/

Visit my website: https://shylastarr.com/

9 781987 863482